Merthyr Tydfil Public Libraries

Llyfrgelloedd Cyhoeddus Merthyr Tudful

Renew / adnewyddu:

Tel / *Ffon*: 01685 725258

Email / *Ebost*: library.services@merthyr.gov.uk

Catalogue / *Catalogau*: http://capitadiscovery.co.uk/merthyr/

1 9 NOV 2018	
2 5 OCT 2018	

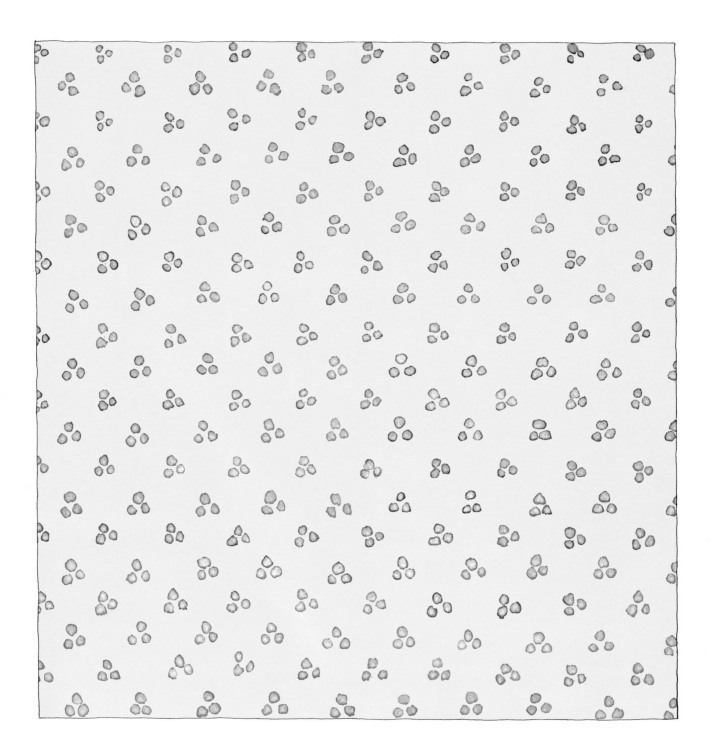

For Sarah and Richard

First published 1985 by Walker Books Ltd
87 Vauxhall Walk, London SE11 5HJ

This edition published 2003

2 4 6 8 10 9 7 5 3 1

© 1985 Helen Craig Ltd

The right of Helen Craig to be identified as author/illustrator of this work has been
asserted by her in accordance with the Copyright, Designs and Patents Act 1988

This book has been typeset in M Baskerville

Printed in China

British Library Cataloguing in Publication Data:
a catalogue record for this book is available from the British Library

ISBN 0-7445-9458-8

The Knight, the Princess and the Dragon

HELEN CRAIG

WALKER BOOKS
AND SUBSIDIARIES
LONDON • BOSTON • SYDNEY

Susie and Alfred were neighbours.
They were also best friends.

One summer holiday they were invited to stay
with Susie's Aunty Bess and Uncle Jonas.

One day Uncle Jonas took them to a picture gallery.
The picture that Susie and Alfred liked best showed
a knight saving a princess from a dreadful dragon.

On the way home Susie wondered if Alfred loved her
enough to save her from a dragon. The more she wondered,
the more she worried. So she decided to find out.

The next day Alfred heard shouts from the
apple tree. It was Susie. "Help! Help! I'm stuck!"
"Nonsense," said Alfred, "I'm busy. Come down
the way you went up!"

"Oh, dear," thought Susie. "Alfred doesn't
seem to care for me any more."

She thought awhile and then set off across
the pond in Uncle Jonas's boat.

In the middle of the pond Susie started to scream.
"Help! Help! There's a TERRIBLE HORRIBLE
SEA SERPENT coming to eat me up!"
Alfred looked up. "Wait a moment, I'm still busy.
I can't come yet."

Susie felt miserable. She was sure
that Alfred loved someone else,
perhaps prettier than her.

So she ran to her bedroom to dress up.

"Now I am a beautiful princess," she told her reflection in the mirror. "I'm sure Alfred will come and save me."

Picking up her skirts, which were a bit too long,
she climbed the stairs to her castle …

and made her way to the balcony to look for Alfred.

Just then she felt that something terrible
was close by. She looked up, and there
above her head was a REAL DRAGON!

"Goodness me!" she gasped, and fell off the balcony …

right on top of a roaring, snorting creature.

"Oh, no! Another monster!" wailed Susie.

"Not at all," puffed the creature, adjusting its home-made helmet. "Sir Alfred the Knight at your service. Did I hear you mention a monster?"

"Yes, yes. Please save me, dear Sir Alfred!" cried Susie.
"There's a real dragon up in the loft. I promise
   I'm not imagining it."

"Leave it to me," said Sir Alfred, picking up his lance and shield.

Susie was too scared to go with him and she hid
while Alfred crept up the stairs.

He burst into the loft with a blood-curdling yell
and attacked the dragon. The strings holding
Uncle Jonas's stuffed crocodile snapped, and it
fell to the floor. Then the battle began …

with a THUD
and an OUCH …

with a CRASH
and a BUMP …

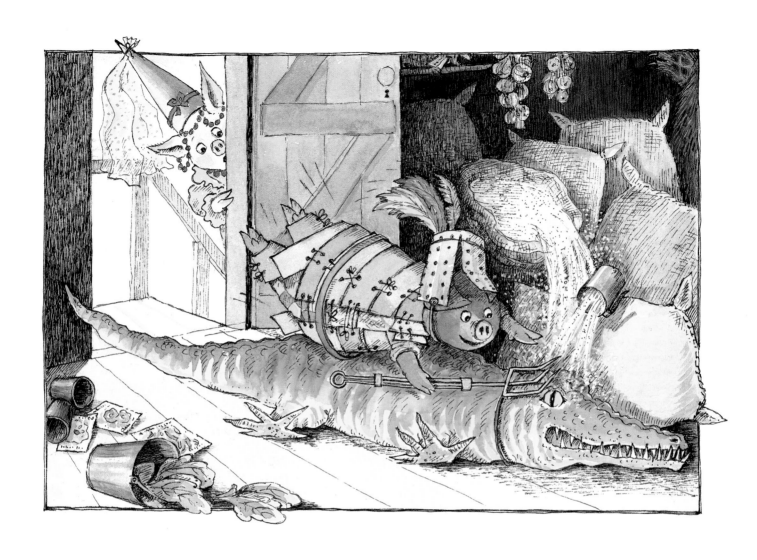

and a BANG!

"Oh, thank you Sir Alfred, I hope you are not hurt."

"It was nothing," said Alfred. "Any time you need
saving, madam, just call on me."

All summer they played with the dragon. Sometimes
Alfred rescued Susie, but quite often she rescued him!

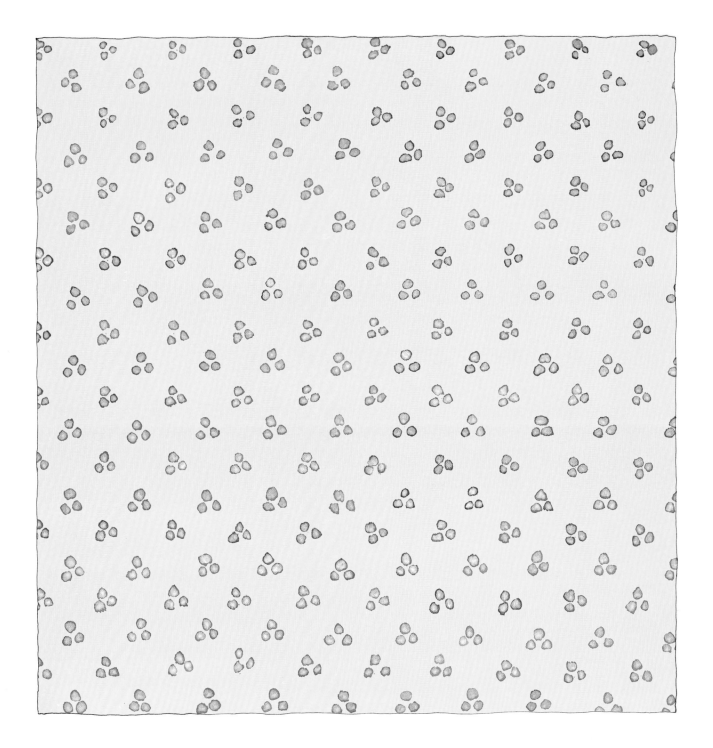